Pick It Up

and

Pup!

Maverick
Early Readers

'Pick It Up' and 'Pup!'
An original concept by Jenny Jinks
© Jenny Jinks

Illustrated by Jessica Morichi

Published by MAVERICK ARTS PUBLISHING LTD
Studio 11, City Business Centre, 6 Brighton Road,
Horsham, West Sussex, RH13 5BB
© Maverick Arts Publishing Limited August 2021
+44 (0)1403 256941

A CIP catalogue record for this book is available at the British Library.

ISBN 978-1-84886-808-3

www.maverickbooks.co.uk

This book is rated as: Pink Band (Guided Reading)
It follows the requirements for Phase 2 phonics.
Most words are decodable, and any non-decodable words are familiar,
supported by the context and/or represented in the artwork.

Pick It Up

and

Pup!

By
Jenny Jinks

Illustrated by
Jessica Morichi

The Letter P

Trace the lower and upper case letter with a finger. Sound out the letter.

Down,
up,
around

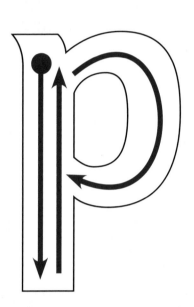

Down,
up,
around

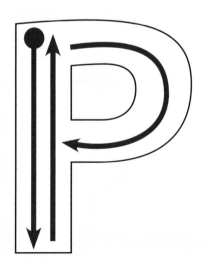

Some words to familiarise:

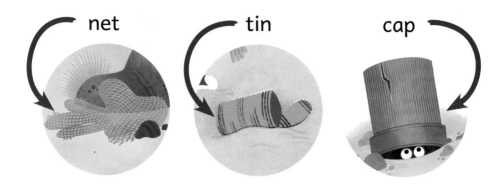

net tin cap

High-frequency words:

is   on   a   it   I   up

Tips for Reading 'Pick It Up'

- Practise the words listed above before reading the story.

- If the reader struggles with any of the other words, ask them to look for sounds they know in the word. Encourage them to sound out the words and help them read the words if necessary.

- After reading the story, ask the reader why Ben put the cap back.

Fun Activity

Discuss other things a hermit crab might live in.

Pick It Up

Ben is on a run.

It is a net.

It is a tin.

It is a bag.

It is a cap.

The Letter U

Trace the lower and upper case letter with a finger. Sound out the letter.

Down,
around,
up,
down

Down,
around,
up

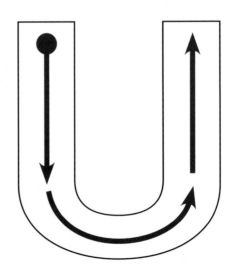

Some words to familiarise:

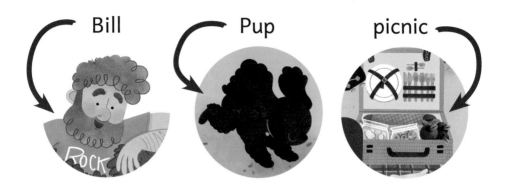

Bill   Pup   picnic

High-frequency words:

go   on   a   it   is

Tips for Reading 'Pup!'

- Practise the words listed above before reading the story.

- If the reader struggles with any of the other words, ask them to look for sounds they know in the word. Encourage them to sound out the words and help them read the words if necessary.

- After reading the story, ask the reader where Pup had been hiding.

Fun Activity

Discuss what you would take on a picnic.

Pup!

Bill and Pup go
on a picnic.

Run, run, run!

It is not Pup. It is a cat.

It is not Pup. It is a bag.

26

It is not Pup. It is a hat.

Bill is sad.

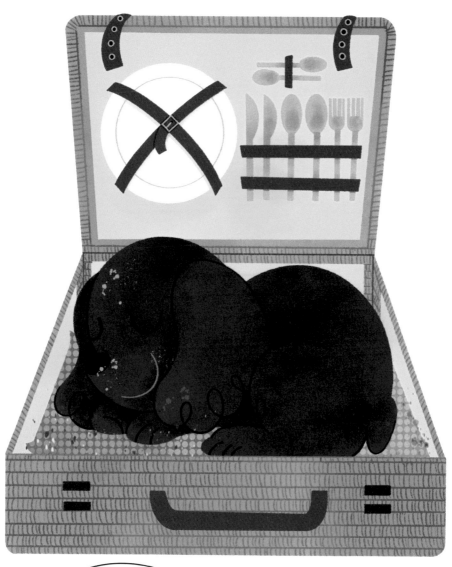

Pup!

Book Bands for Guided Reading

The Institute of Education book banding system is a scale of colours that reflects the various levels of reading difficulty. The bands are assigned by taking into account the content, the language style, the layout and phonics. Word, phrase and sentence level work is also taken into consideration.

Maverick Early Readers are a bright, attractive range of books covering the pink to white bands. All of these books have been book banded for guided reading to the industry standard and edited by a leading educational consultant.

To view the whole Maverick Readers scheme, visit our website at www.maverickearlyreaders.com

Or scan the QR code above to view our scheme instantly!